VENGEANCE
& FORGIVENESS

VENGEANCE & FORGIVENESS

BY VINCENT A. PICCONE, M.D.

ReadersMagnet, LLC

INTRODUCTION

To forgive is to grant free pardon for or remission of an offense, to pardon an offense or an offender, to give up all claim on account of an injury. God expects us not only to give up vengeance against other people but to forgive them from the heart for whatever they have done to injure us. Even further God expects us to love, pray for, bless, and do good to our enemies. This is a basic of the Christian message, and what separates us from all other peoples. When we do this all the ill will and negativism on our part disappears and we are free to concentrate on more constructive relationships both with our enemies and ourselves. While we may not change the feelings of our enemies this method to deal with human relationships allows us to be at peace with ourselves. Sometimes if we are lucky enough, our enemies turn into friends.

Everyone has enemies and we all will have many during our lives. Our enemies mistreat us, slander us, injure us emotionally and sometimes physically, and even seek to kill us. Our first response is to want to do to them even worse than what they have done to us. We seek revenge. Why do we have enemies? Sometimes our enemies may be sent to us from God so that we will change our behavior."When the Lord is pleased with a man's ways, he makes even his enemies at peace with him (proverbs 16:7). Enemies might covet or envy what we have or be jealous. We might have committed slights or offenses against others without awareness of that fact and incited their wrath. There may be a conflict between good and evil. Miscommunication may have led to conflict. There might be a natural competition for limited resources that incites anger. Religious, ethnic, or racial differences might give rise to animosities. Differences in physical characteristics may lead to hatred and anger between people. The reasons to have enemies are indeed many.

To deal with our enemies in a better fashion we must first analyze what they have done to injure us. When we believe we are slandered the first thing to do is separate truth from falsity in our enemies speech. Often there are elements of truth in what they say. These truths in their speech as faults in our character must be addressed and corrected if possible. Our enemies can find our weak points and theses are areas we must strengthen ourselves. Why are enemies good to have? They expose our faults and weaknesses so that we can improve ourselves. If we are called fat and we are fat, if it bothers us we should lose weight. To seek vengeance will not make us any thinner!

Never trusting your enemies and to keep your distance from them is always good advice.

There is a natural tendency among people to return anger, hurt, violence, malice, and many more negative experiences on those who they perceived instigated these against them in the first place- to return tit for tat, injury for injury, stripe for stripe. People need to return evil upon those who initiated it against them. A cycle can develop where the person who initiated the first injury, after he catches the anger of his victim, and himself is injured, returns more negativity in the form of words or actions. After a while it looks from a different perspective like two people who hit each other over their heads with sledge hammers. There is a cycle of violence between the two parties that does not cease. It is often impossible when these cycles are initiated to determine who fired the first shot, or even if that matters when the cycle of hatred is engaged. Vengeance is part of the human heart. This dynamic is seen between marriage partners, co-workers, enemies, family members and just about everyone.

War has many causes, economic, social, religious etc. Often when a war stops, after a period of peace, a new war is initiated to avenge the party that lost the first war. A cycle of war develops that is difficult to stop. Whether it be African tribes, or European countries, or hindu-islamic violence there is an endless cycle of retribution, and counter violence. In some sense war can be seen as group vengeance. The nations of the world engage in group tit for tat, stripe for stripe- injury for injury.

War and human vengeance make some sense from a odd point of view. If we injure those who injure us they might be less likely, less willing, and less able to injure us back. They will think twice if injured to repeat their evil upon us. Indeed sometimes when wars are not deliberately planned,"military preparation" is often seen as a means to avoid war. No-body wants to battle people with a strong military for fear that they may lose a war. On the other hand if the human mind and human heart are as firmly set in revenge as history records, then their retribution may be more likely, more able, and more willed.

The concept of vengeance is particularly of interest when one discusses enemies. An enemy is typically one who seeks to destroy or injure the object of their hate. The enemy seeks injury and the injured party seeks retribution; again tit for tat, injury for injury, tit for tat.

For thousands of years, war and vengeance raged, as they do even today. The cost has been enormous in terms of human injury, human suffering, human death, property damage and the like. The cost has also been diversion of resources from peaceful uses and increased strife among people and nations. In a nuclear age human war and vengeance can result in the destruction of mankind himself and the destruction of the world.

With the advent of Jesus Christ, we are given as humans, a new command. Instead of vengeance and war we are to seek forgiveness and peace. Discord is replaced with harmony and hatred with love. This book seeks to explain the teachings of Jesus with regard to enemies and warfare. It is meant to contrast the laws of the old testament with the teaching of the new testament. More importantly the book seeks to give people an example with which to live their lives. The teaching of the book of psalms is illustrative-"Do not be provoked by evildoers, and do not envy those who do wrong, Like grass they wither quickly; like green plants they wither away. Do not be provoked by the prosperous, nor by malicious schemers. Give up anger, abandon your wrath, it brings only harm. Those who do evil will be cut off." (Psalm 37). Jesus taught not to return evil for evil- either individually or as a group.

Never trusting your enemies and to keep your distance from them is always good advice.

"But to you who hear I say, love your enemies, do good to those who hate you, bless those who curse you, pray for those who mistreat you. To the person who strikes you on one cheek, offer the other as well, and from the one who takes your cloak, do not withhold even your tunic. Give to everyone who asks of you, and from the one who takes what is yours, do not demand it back."

Luke 6: 27-30

Jesus tells us how to seek vengeance on our enemies; treat them the way we would want to be treated, the Golden rule. We seek no vengeance on our enemies, we return no ill will; we love our enemies, go good to them, bless them, and pray for them.

When a group of people is slighted against or injured by another group, the same dynamic holds- the group that is injured can collectively forgive the group that causes the injury. Reparations are not sought by the injured group and vengeance is left up to God. This way to deal with injury avoids war. When a group of people collectively leave their fate up to God, they put they future in good hands.

Patient perseverance of a group of people in the face of repeated hostility by another group is difficult but war can be far more destructive and difficult. With prayer sometimes the aggressor will abandon their aggression. The meek shall inherit the earth.

" You shall not bear hatred for your brother in your heart. Though you may have to reprove neighbor your fellow man, do not incur sin because of him. Take no revenge and cherish no grudge against your fellow countryman. You shall love your neighbor as yourself. I am the Lord."

Leviticus 19:17-18

Here the term brother refers to anyone we know and not just a family member. The emphasis is on the fact that they should not be hated. Hatred should not be born against any person. Hatred is a dangerous emotion, one that consumes time and emotional and physical energy. It leads to strife, bloodshed, and murder. It is alright to chastise your neighbor or tell a reason you are at odds with him in an attempt to correct a misunderstanding but anything beyond this asks for trouble.

We are told by this old testament command that we should not take revenge against anyone. When a person feels slighted or injured by someone else the reasons can be many. A misunderstanding, a mistake, or even an accident could have led to some disagreement. A tendency to revenge when resisted can dampen or eliminate the ping pong effect of reprisal followed by reprisal. Arguments and hostilities are de-escalated and peace is restored.

*****

People might think that they have a right to revenge a thought that is perpetuated in popular culture. However everything that God says about revenge is the exact opposite. Revenge should be left to God. Only God can see the heart of someone and know the full story and the exact reasons why people may apparently act out against another.

*****

With lex talionis- the law of tit for tat, everyone ends up blind or at least injured. Restraint from vengeful behavior- meekness- is rewarded by peace and tranquility. Those who sow peace and tranquility are rewarded by peace and tranquility. A main difference between Christianity and all other people is a love of enemies.

We know the one who said:"Vengeance is mine; I will repay," and again:"The Lord will judge his people," It is a fearful thing to fall into the hands of the living God.

Hebrew 10:30-31

When we seek vengeance against people we must be sure it is well deserved. If we have incited people to act against us, if we have caused other people pain and suffering, if we have acted against people without provocation we very well deserve a hostile reaction. Any reaction against this hostility reaction is not appropriate. We reap what we sow.

If on the other hand we have not injured people, have treated them as we would want to be treated, and have been neighborly, and people try to destroy us and act as enemies towards us then we might think that revenge is justified. In this case the new testament letters and gospel state that we should not react in anger or seek revenge but leave the situation up to God who will apply an appropriate vengeance on these people.

God gives several examples of his vengeance in the bible" You shall not molest or oppress an alien, for you were once aliens yourselves in the land of Egypt. You shall not wrong any widow or orphan. If ever you wrong them and they cry out to me, I will surely hear their cry. My wrath will flare up, and I will kill you with the sword; then your own wives will be widows, and you children orphans."

God's retribution is well described and codified for various personal injuries in the lex talionis, the law of tit for tat. This law was meant to enforce strict punishment for various offenses but also to limit then so they would not be more severe than the offense merited.

Leave vengeance and wrath and judgment up to God! God has the ability to punish in this world and the next and can serve our enemies the just desserts they deserve far better than we can.

"You have heard that it was said 'An eye for an eye and a tooth for a tooth.' But I say to you, offer no resistance to one who is evil. When someone strikes you on your right cheek, turn the other one to him as well. If anyone wants to go to law with you over your tunic, hand him your cloak as well. Should anyone press you into service for one mile," Go with him for two miles. Give to the one who asks of you, and do not turn your back on the one who wants to borrow."

Matthew 5:38-42

****

Never trust your enemy, for his wickedness is like corrosion in bronze. Even though he acts humbly and peaceable toward you, take care to be on your guard against him. Rub him as one polishes a brazen mirror, and you will find that there is still corrosion. Let him not stand near you, lest he oust you and take your place. Let him not sit at your right hand, lest he then demand your seat, And in the end you appreciate my advice, when you groan with regret, as I warned you. Who pities a snake charmer when he is bitten, and anyone who goes near a wild beast? So it is with the companion of the proud man, who is involved in his sins; While you stand firm, he makes no bold move, but if you slip, he cannot hold back. While his lips an enemy speaks sweetly, but in his heart he schemes to plunge you into the abyss. Though your enemy has tears in his eyes, if given the chance, he will never have enough of your blood. If evil comes upon you, you will find him at hand; feigning to help, he will trip you up. Then he will nod his head and clap his hands and hiss repeatedly, and show his true face.

Sirach 12: 10-18

Keep away from your enemies; be on guard with your friends.

SIRACH

It is common to want to seek vengeance against our enemies especially if they have done us harm. There are some reasons however that we might not seek vengeance. The enemy might become so angry with us when we have been vengeful that they might seek to kill us. Vengeance against our enemies might also create a ping-pong effect so that, alternatively we injure them and they come back to injure us in further retaliation. Our enemy might also hire attorneys against us and bring us to court where we might lose wealth in costly litigation.

The Gospels tell us to love our enemies, pray for them, do good to them, and bless them. This goes against human nature. While we can do all these things it is probably still best that we keep away from them as much as possible so they can not directly injure us. There is still the possibility that the dynamics of the relationship might change and that they might become friendlier or even become friends. Even more against human nature is God's call to forgive our enemies. It is only with forgiveness that we can separate ourselves from the destructive rut caused by the mutual destruction caused when we seek vengeance against one another.

Human vengeance and anger does not serve God's vengeance or serve his sense of justice. When you seek vengeance against your enemy, hold back. You will find that if you wait, and if vengeance is truly deserved, that God can dole out the vengeance with far greater effect and intensity than you could ever. God scrutinizes relationships and is able to set things right in our eyes far better than we can.

"Say not," As he did to me, so will I do to him; I will repay him according to his deeds"

Proverbs 24:29

"Say not,"I will repay evil!" Trust in the Lord and he will help you"

Proverbs 20:22

These two bible quotations make it quite clear that we are not to seek vengeance. If a man slaps your face you are not to slap his face, and if he crashes into you car purposefully you should not smash into his car. One is not to do to our enemies what they did to us. We should not retaliate but put the situation in God's hands who will do justice for us if we allow him to. Again, the wrath of man does not accomplish the righteousness of God.

What should one do then if an enemy hurts them? Nothing! One should not under any circumstances return any evil whatsoever. If need be and if you are able to keep away from your enemy but do not injure them in return.

What does trust in the Lord and he will help you mean? It means that we should give up any intention to seek retribution and let all action against the injuring party be left up to God. God in his own time and his own manner will repay our enemy the payback.

When we leave vengeance up to God we suffer no guilt that we have done something wrong and we suffer no worry that we overdid the revenge because God imposed his justice not us. And, after God serves the vengeance we can think back and believe that the vengeance God served up was perfect for that situation.

Sometimes we might get paranoid when someone supposedly does something that appears harmful to us but is well intended. Sometimes people do things to us to reprove us or improve us but we consider to be ill intended. When we attack people it causes then to refrain from continued efforts to improve or reprove us, and this can hurt us. Sometimes God too can cause events in our lives through other people to unfold that he means to teach us a lesson but we consider very harmful to us. When we lash out at other people it interferes with the plan of God to teach us something about our lives. Only in retrospect can we see that our anger and retribution hurt someone who meant to help us.

So too when we seek revenge against our enemies and do to them what they did to us it can make us look immature or even mean spirited. Who wants to have anything to do with someone who slaps you right back in the face when they slap you. You appear short tempered. Then too if we seek vengeance against our enemies then they might want to get us worse the second time or we might get caught up in a vicious cycle of harm that ping pongs back and forth between two parties.

"He who digs a pit falls into it; and a stone comes back upon him who rolls it."

Proverbs 26:27

"He who digs a pit may fall into it."

Ecclesiastes 10:8

" A stone falls back on him who throws it up, so a blow struck in treachery injures more than one. And he who digs a pit falls into it, and he who lays a snare is caught in it. Whoever does harm will be involved in it, without knowing how it came upon him".

Sirach 27:25-27

There is no need to seek vengeance against your enemies, for by their words and actions our enemies destroy themselves. By the pits they dig, the snares they lay, and the stones they throw our enemies injure themselves. All people of good will and called by the Lord have to do is seek the protection of the Lord and allow their enemies to do to themselves (the enemies) what they intended to do to the people of goodwill.

As enemies scheme to destroy Christian or Jewish people they actually plot their own destruction.

" Sinners conceive iniquity; pregnant with mischief, they give birth to failure. They open a hole and dig it deep, but fall into the pit that they have dug. Their mischief comes back upon themselves; their violence falls on their own heads."

Psalm 7:15-17

" The nations fall into the pit they dig; in the snare they hide, their own foot is caught. The Lord is revealed by this divine rule: by the deeds they do the wicked are trapped."

Psalm 9:16-17

"Repay them for their deeds, for the evil that they do. For the work of their hands repay them; give them what they deserve"

Psalm 28:4

"Let ruin overtake them awares; let the snare they have set catch them; let them fall into the pit they have dug"

Psalm 35:8

" The wicked draw their swords; they string their bows To fell the poor and oppressed, to slaughter those whose way is honest. Their swords will pierce their own hearts; their bows will be broken."

Psalm 37: 14-15

"They have set a trap for my feet; my soul is bowed down; They have dug a pit before me, may they fall into it themselves!"

Psalm 57:7

"But those who seek my life will come to ruin; they shall go down to the depths of the earth! They shall be handed over to the sword and become the prey of Jackals!"

Psalm 63: 10-11

"But God will shoot arrows at them and strike them unawares. They will be brought down by their own tongues"

Psalm 64: 8-9

The old testament is full of yearnings of the human heart for revenge against our enemies. The old testament asks God to avenge us for the injuries caused to us by our enemies. However the vengeance is limited to them suffering what they intended us to suffer. It does not lessen or amplify the pain and suffering they sought to inflict on us. The new testament teaching of Jesus however tells us to love, do good, bless, and pray for our enemies and let the vengeance up to God.

"In our prosperity we cannot know our friends; in adversity an enemy will not remain concealed. When a man is successful even his friend is friendly; in adversity even his friend disappears. Never trust your enemy, for his wickedness is like corrosion in bronze. Even though he acts humbly and peaceably towards you, take care to be on your guard against him. Rub him as one polishes a brazen mirror, and you will find that there is still corrosion. Let him not stand near you, lest he oust you and take your place. Let him not sit at your right hand, lest he then demand your seat, And in the end you appreciate my advice, when you groan with regret as I warned you. Who pities a snake charmer when he is bitten, or anyone who goes near a wild beast? So with the companion of a proud man who is involved in his sins: While you stand firm, he makes no bold move; but if you slip he cannot hold back. With his lips an enemy speaks sweetly, but in his heart he schemes to plunge you into the abyss. Though your enemy has tears in his eyes, if given the chance, he will never have enough of your blood. IF evil comes upon you, you will find him at hand; feigning to help, he will trip you up. Then he will nod his head and clap his hands, and hiss repeatedly, and show his true face."

Sirach 12: 8-18

Everyone has enemies and we all will have many during our lives. Our enemies mistreat us slander us, injure us emotionally and sometimes physically, and even seek to kill us. Our first response is to want to do to them even worse that what they have done to us. We seek revenge.

The old testament give us some advice on how to recognize and deal with enemies. The Book of Sirach has much to say about enemies. Never trusting your enemies and to keep your distance from them is always good advice.

To deal with our enemies in a better fashion we must first analyze what they have dome to injure us. When we believe we are slandered the first thing to do is separate truth from falsity in our enemies speech. Often there are elements of truth in what they say. These truths in their speech, as faults in our character must be addressed and corrected if possible. Our enemies can find weak points and these are areas we must strengthen ourselves. If we are called fat, and if that bothers us we should lose weight. To seek vengeance in any other manner will not make us thinner.

" Say not,"As he did to me, so will I do to him; I will repay him according to his deeds"

Proverbs 24:29

"Say not I will repay evil" Trust in the Lord and he will help you"

Proverbs 20:22

These two bible verses make it quite clear that we are not to seek vengeance. If a man slaps your face you are not to slap his face, and if he crashes into your car purposefully you should not smash into his car. One is not to do to our enemies what they did to us. We should not retaliate but put the situation in God's hands who will do justice for us if we allow him to. Again, the wrath of man does not accomplish the righteousness of God.

What should one do then if an enemy hurts them? Nothing! One should not under any circumstances return any evil whatsoever. If need be, and if you can, you should keep away from them but do not injure them in return.

What does"trust in the Lord, and he will help you" mean? It means that we should give up any intention to seek retribution and let all action against the injuring party be left up to God. God in his own time and in his own manner will repay the enemy the payback.

When we leave vengeance up to God we suffer no guilt that we have done something wrong and we suffer no worry that we overdid the revenge because God imposed the vengeance not us. And, after God serves the vengeance we can think back and believe that the vengeance God served up was perfect for that situation.

Sometimes we might get paranoid when someone supposedly does something that appears harmful to us but is well intended. Sometimes people do things to us to reprove or improve us but we consider to be ill intended. When we attack people it causes them to refrain from continues efforts to improve or reprove us, and this can hurt us. Sometimes God, too, can cause events in our lives through other people to unfold that he means to teach us a lesson but we consider to be very harmful to us. When we lash out at other people it interferes with the plan of God to teach us something about our lives, Only in retrospect can we see that our anger and retribution hurt someone who meant to help us.

So too when we seek revenge against our enemies and do to them what they did to us it can make us look immature or even mean spirited. Who wants to have anything to do with someone who slaps you right back in the face when they slap you? You appear short tempered. Then too if we seek vengeance against our enemies then they might want to get us worse the second time or we might get caught up in a vicious cycle of harm that ping pongs back and forth between the two parties.

Many wars are caused as a result of poor conclusions to previous wars. When impossible demands are made on the vanquished then it is quite possible to see that the vanquished will again fight to throw off the yoke of the victor.

" Do not think that I have come to bring peace upon the earth. I have come to bring not peace but the sword. For I have come to set a man 'against his father, a daughter against her mother, and a daughter in law against her mother-in-law; and one's enemies will be those of his household.'"

Matthew 10:34-36

The Christian mission Jesus sends us on into the world is more important than our families. Our families will hate us if we try to bring the teachings of Jesus into the world. As the world hates Jesus message so it will hate those who carry the message to the world. Our enemies

Ancient Israel gives example of how God can intervene in war according to his purpose. God can aid his allies to win and defeat his enemies. When ancient Israel followed God's commandments and obeyed his laws and worshipped him they were undefeatable in battle; When they disobeyed him , did not follow his laws or obey his commands, or worship him they were defeated. When God wished Ancient Israel to win in battle he sometimes intervened supernaturally.

At Moses command and at the divine intervention of God, God separated the waters of the dead sea and allowed to Israelites to pass to the Sinai peninsula. The Egyptians followed and were drowned.

"Beloved, do not look for revenge but leave room for the wrath; for it is written,"Vengeance is mine, I will repay, says the Lord." Rather," if your enemy is hungry, feed him; if he is thirsty, give him something to drink; for by so doing you will reap burning coals upon his head. Do not be conquered by evil but conquer evil with good."

Romans 12: 19-21

This wisdom is repeated in proverbs chapter 25 verse 21-22" If your enemy be hungry, give him food to eat, if he be thirsty, give him to drink; For live coals you will heap on his head, and the Lord will vindicate you.

Human nature tells us to destroy our enemies or to do them enough harm that they cannot hurt us. There is a certain satisfaction and smugness one gains when we injure our enemies. When we feel we have gotten the better of them, or at least gotten them better than they got us, there is a sense of relief. Like balm on an injury we feel better; at least for a while. Sometimes, later, guilt may creep in or we feel bad about ourselves that we have injured our enemy. This is especially true if we have done irreversible harm to our enemies.

" Or what king marching into battle would not first decide whether with ten thousand troops he can successfully oppose another king advancing upon him with twenty thousand troops? But if not, while he is still far away, he will send a delegation to ask for peace terms."

Luke 14:31-32

1 Corinthians 6: 7

"Now indeed [Then} it is, in any case, a failure on your part that you have lawsuits against one another. Why not rather put up with injustice? Why not rather let yourselves be cheated?"

" Our Father in heaven, hallowed be your name, your kingdom come, your will be done, on earth as in heaven. Give us today our daily bread; and forgive us our debts, as we forgive our debtors; and do not subject us to the final test, but deliver us from the evil one.'"" If you forgive others their transgressions, your heavenly father will forgive you. But if you do not forgive others neither will your father forgive your transgressions."

Matthew 6:9-13

The word of God is clear. Not only must we refrain from vengeance against our enemies but we must also forgive them their trespasses against us. This goes beyond the simple task of not seeking vengeance against our enemies. Unless we do this God will not forgive us our trespasses against others. Also, if we do not forgive our enemies the grudges we hold against them it is highly unlikely that those who hold grudges against us will forgive us. The cycle of animosities, angers, and hurts that can overwhelm our lives will never stop unless we forgive our enemies. Holding grudges is bad physically and mentally for us. When we forgive others we satisfy the Golden Rule treat others the way we would want to be treated we create a better life for ourselves. We stop ruminating over past hurts and this allows us to get on in our lives. Our lives are not consumed by tit for tat and we do not have to worry about when the next blow or hurt will come from. Forgiveness of others transgressions brings peace to our lives. It also is in compliance with the command by Jesus to love one another. Even more possible when we forgive our neighbors our trespasses we might even make a friend.

The book of proverbs in the Bible states that when the Lord is pleased with a man's ways, he makes even his enemies be at peace with him. A man can only please the Lord if he forgives his enemies in addition to other factors. Another point about forgiving our enemies is that God will not forgive us our trespasses, unless we forgive those who trespass against us and without God's forgiveness we sacrifice Heaven. Certainly unless we learn to forgive those who trespass against us we are not ready for heaven. The man who holds and bears grudges is not fit for the kingdom of God.

Sometimes we trespass against God in our words or actions. When we pray to God to ask him to forgive our trespasses against him is he not aware how we have dealt with our neighbor? We in fact are hypocrites as we seek forgiveness of our transgressions against him, but are unwilling to extend our forgiveness to our neighbors and our enemies.

We are allowed to be temporarily angry with our neighbors when they cause us injury-"be angry but do not sin. Do not let the sun set on your anger." Retaliation is out of the question. This is the only path to peace and tranquility of mind that we will find. When we forgive others we are forgiven.

"Blessed are the meek, for they shall inherit the land."

Matthew 5:5

Meekness is humble patience or submission as under provocation from others, as opposed to vengeance or retaliation when provoked. Rather than retaliation or vengeance one accepts the taunts, insults, and intimidations of others without reaction to them. Those who do this are promised by Jesus himself to inherit the land.

THE VENGEANCE OF GOD

We are the creature and God is the Creator. God has made us and given us specific laws to follow. The laws are meant to ensure our survival and be to our benefit. However when we disobey God's laws we are sure to be punished either in this life or the next, by God. While God is a loving God he is also vengeful toward's those who disobey his laws and commandments.

What causes madness in this life is that some people are not always punished or punished immediately when they break laws and commandments. This is because there is another force in the universe, the devil. The devil sometimes protects people against

God's wrath in return for their allegiance to the devil. God allows this as he knows that these people will be punished in the next world ie. hell. After all we are creatures given free choice- given the choice between good and evil. To choose between God the Devil. God respects this choice.

Again, there are times when God takes his time in punishing us to give us time to repent of our transgressions. But when we break God's commandments we are sure to get it sooner or later.

When Jesus died on the cross he conquered death forever, however he did not annihilate the devil at that time. Only at the end of the age will Jesus cast down satan forever, and people be judged on how well they kept God's commandments.

God's judgment extends to this world then, and the next. With God's vengeance there is also forgiveness. If we give up our transgressions and repent and forsake previous behaviors we are sure to be forgiven by God. There is no vengeance of human's against God for God is not susceptible to man's vengeance.

Examples of God's vengeance are found throughout the New and Old testaments. God punished Cain when he killed his brother Able as he banished him from the soil. God punished David for Killing Uriah and taking his wife. God killed king Saul and his son's as he did not follow God's instructions. Jesus angered at the money changers in the temple overturned their tables.

When we disobey God's rules and commandments we are sure to reap God's vengeance. To think that we can avoid his wrath is foolhardy. Sometimes God's vengeance is subdued as he allows us to destroy ourselves by our own actions and sometimes he is active in our destruction. The algorithm is simple we are forgiven when we seek forgiveness and we suffer God's wrath we break his rules and commandments. Is this fair? God designed us and made us with intrinsic fallibilities that can only be managed as we follow God's rules and regulations. If we do not follow these we are destroyed. Whether it be an adulterous man who is shot by an angry husband, a murderer who gets the death penalty, or a man who is disinherited because he did not honor his parents God's vengeance is always there and cannot be avoided or appealed.

OF WAR

War is by nature destructive of both property and people. Property gets destroyed and people get injured and killed. The damage is often irreparable and unrepairable. Sometimes the damage caused to people and property in war exceeds that than if the party that would have to defend itself had just surrendered. The party that is called to defend itself also must

Old Testament Vengefulness

Vengeance is defined as the avenging of wrong, injury or the like, or retributive punishment. The old testament is replete with acts of vengeance by both man and God. The wisdom of God and the wisdom of man often led to greatly different ends.

When God sees how wicked men are prior to the flood he decides to destroy all mankind except for Noah and his relatives. He send the flood and all mankind is destroyed except for those on the ark. God sent the flood to cleanse the human race of evil. With God's vengefulness there was no second chance and no exceptions. God acted with finality and clarity of purpose.

Lot lived in the city of Sodom which became notoriously wicked. God sent two angels to destroy all of Sodom, Gomorrah, and the whole region of the plain. Only Lot and his two daughters were saved. Again God saw wickedness and destroyed those who practiced it. God's vengefulness was un-appealable and complete.

The rape of Dinah in the book of Genesis provides an example of human vengefulness. Dinah is raped by Shechem of a tribe different from that of Jacob and his family. When Jacob's sons learn of it they become angry and slaughter all of Shechem's clan. Jacob reproaches his sons as they have exposed the family to possible harm from the local inhabitants. Jacob's family could have been wiped out if the local tribes united and attacked Jacob's family. In this instance vengefulness could have been the destruction of the patriarch's family.

Sampson, judge of Israel is surrounded by the pagan Philistines, who worshiped a foreign god. He chose a Philistine woman, however to be his wife. When another man marries her before him he becomes angry and burns the land of the Philistines by tying together the tails of foxes, with torches attached. Later he sought the company of Delilah. Delilah has him bound and blinded by the Philistines. Later he destroys these enemies of Israel by pushing apart the columns of the Philistine temple killing all the Philistine lords.

In the first instance Samson acted vengefully on his own behalf. In the second incident he acted on God's behalf to kill the Philistines. The Philistines were killed because they followed false Gods.

King David also suffered from the vengeance of God. David took Bathsheba, another man's wife, and had sex with her and she became pregnant. David had the woman's husband killed in battle and took the woman for his own wife. God retaliated by bring evil to David's house and promising that evil would never part from his house.

PEACE

"Peace be with you"
John 20:19
"Peace be with you"
John 20:21
"Peace be with you"
John 20:26

"Peace I leave with you; my peace I give to you. Not as the world gives do I give it to you. Do not let your hearts be troubled or afraid."

John 14:27

There is a saying"know Jesus, know peace-no Jesus, no peace". The heart of this saying is true-without Jesus there can be no peace. Peace is defined as freedom from war or hostilities. The peace defined by Jesus however is tranquility of heart and mind. Only if a country is truly and thoroughly Christian can it achieve peace. The commandment to treat others they way you want to be treated when followed by many can lead to peace. Jesus teaching of love of enemies, do good to those who hate you, bless those who curse you, and pray for those who mistreat you results in peace. It is basic human psychology that people do not want to destroy or kill those who treat them well even if initially they were enemies or hated by them.

Jesus statement"Peace be with you" was applied individually and collectively to a group of people. Presumably it can be applied collectively to many people who follow Jesus's commands or even to a nation. Perhaps when people collectively turn the other cheek when struck on one side; when they go the extra mile when pressed into one; when they do not turn their back on the one who wants to borrow and give to those who ask; and who collectively offer their tunics when people demand their cloaks; these people may find peace.

Countries spend their treasures and deplete their treasuries to buy arms and armies to protect them when in fact it is only God that can save and protect them. If they spent a small fraction of what they spend on arms on good will then they might have peace. Arms buildups by one country are often followed by arms buildups by other countries. The cycle can be vicious and consume all the wealth of several nations. And, what good are all these armaments unless they are used!

Some people believe that if you want peace you must prepare for the eventuality of war. If only countries spent as detailed and costly for peace as they did for war then they might have peace. If people shared natural resources, shared food, shared water, shared clothing manufacturing, and honestly strived for peace then they might in fact have peace.

Peace between countries comes from the will sublimation of hostilities and hatreds, angers and differences. Peace comes from group attempts to find common ground, to resolve differences, and find systems of mutual support.

"When the Lord is pleased with a man's ways, he makes even his enemies be at peace with him"

Proverbs 16:7

Then I saw the heavens opened, and there was a white horse; its rider was [called]"Faithful and True." His eyes were [like] a fiery flame, and on his head were many diadems. He had a name inscribed that no one knows except himself. He wore a cloak that had been dipped in blood and his name was called the Word of God. The armies of heaven followed him, mounted on white horses and wearing clean white linen. Out of his mouth came a sharp sword to strike the nations. He will rule them with an iron rod, and he himself will tread out in the wine press the wine of the fury and wrath of God the almighty. He has a name written on his cloak and on his thigh,"King of kings and Lord of Lords."

Then I saw an angel standing on the sun. He cried out [in] a loud voice to all the birds flying high overhead,"Come here. Gather for God's great feast, to eat the flesh of kings, the flesh of military officers, and the flesh of warriors, the flesh of horses and of their riders, and the flesh of all free and slave, small and great." Then I saw the beast and the kings of the earth and their armies gathered to fight against the one riding the horse and against his army. The beast was caught and with it the false prophet who had performed in its sight the signs by which he led astray those who had accepted the mark of the beast and those who had worshipped its image. The two were thrown alive into the fiery pool burning with sulfur. The rest were killed by the sword that came out of the mouth of the one riding the horse, and the birds gorged themselves on their flesh.

Revelation 19:11-21

"When you hear of wars and reports of wars do not be alarmed; such things must happen, but it will not yet be the end."

Mark 13:7

" You will hear of wars and reports of wars; see that you are not alarmed, for these things must happen, but it will not yet be the end. Nation will rise against nation, and kingdom against kingdom".

Matthew 24: 6-7

" Why do you not judge for yourselves what is right. If you are to go with your opponent before a magistrate, make an effort to settle the matter on the way; otherwise your opponent will turn you over to the judge, and the judge hand you over to the constable, and the constable throw you into prison. I say to you, you will not be released until you have paid the last penny."

Luke 12:57-59

"If your brother sins, rebuke him; and if he repents forgive him. And if he wrongs you seven times in one day and returns to you seven times saying, 'I am sorry', you should forgive him."

Luke 17:3-4

The Peter approaching asked him," Lord, if my brother sins against me , how often must I forgive him? As many as seven times? Jesus answered," I say to you, not seven times but seventy seven times. That is why the kingdom of heaven may be likened to a king who decided to settle accounts with his servants. When he began the accounting a debtor was brought before him who owed him a huge amount. Since he had no way of paying it back, his master ordered him to be sold along with his wife, his children, and all his property, in payment of the debt. At that, the servant fell down, did him homage, and said, 'Be patient with me, and I will pay you back in full' Moved with compassion, the master of that servant let him go and forgave him the entire loan. When that servant had left, he found one of his fellow servants who owed him a much smaller amount. He seized him and started to choke him, demanding, 'Pay back what you owe.'. Falling to his knees, his fellow servant begged him, 'Be patient with me and I will pay you back.'. Instead, he had him put in prison until he paid back the debt. Now when his fellow servants saw what had happened, they were deeply disturbed, and went to their master and reported the whole affair. His master summoned him and said to him, 'You wicked servant! I forgave you your entire debt because you begged me to. Should you not have had pity on your fellow servant, as I had pity on you? Then in anger his master handed him over to the torturers until he should pay back the whole debt. So will my heavenly father do to you, unless each of you forgives his brother from his heart."

Matthew 18:21–35

When we go to God for forgiveness he almost always responds with forgiveness of our sins. No matter how bad our transgressions are we find forgiveness. Especially for Catholics in the sacrament of confession, healing and forgiveness is found. It is God's expectation as related by this parable that we will in turn forgive our neighbor's transgressions against us in the same manner God forgives us our transgressions. This is summed up in the our father," forgive us our trespasses as we forgive those who have trespassed against us. God will not forgive us our sins if we do not forgive the sins of other people who sin against us. Blessed are the merciful for they will be shown mercy is another way to relate this parable.

It is interesting that in this parable other people watched carefully what the man did who debt was forgiven by the king. When they found that the forgiven servant was unforgiving they went and relayed the entire affair. People watch us carefully and know whether we are forgiving or not. When our sins are forgiven by God we must be careful to forgive those who have trespassed against us not only to set an example but also because we might be punished for our lack of forgiveness.

Magnitude is also important in this parable. Often many of us have much to be grateful for the many transgression we have against God, when they are forgiven. How much more we must forgive the petty slights that people carry out against. There is a bad spirit in us then we can be forgiven so much yet deny the few forgiveness to the few transgression people carry out against us. God demands us to forgive others.

"The vengeful will suffer the Lord's vengeance for he remembers their sins in detail. Forgive your neighbors injustice; and then when you pray, your own sins will be forgiven. Should a man nourish anger against his fellows, and expect healing from the Lord? Should a man refuse mercy to his fellows yet seek pardon for his own sins? If he who is but flesh cherishes wrath, who will forgive his sins? Remember your last days, set enmity aside; remember death and decay, and cease from sin! Think of the commandments, hate not your neighbor; of the Most High's covenant, and overlook faults."

Sirach 28: 1-7

The old testament is full of prohibitions against revenge and vengeance and this teaching agrees with that of the teaching of Christ. If we are vengeful towards others God will remember our sins and seek vengeance against us. People's inner nature wants to strike out in response to attacks against us; this is human nature. But the teaching of the Judeo-Christian religion is the exact opposite- not to respond in kind. We strike out against our enemy we injure two- both our enemy and ourself.

WAR AND VENGEANCE

Prior to a war there is some provocative event that crystallizes differences between people and leads to the conflict. Wars is usually long in coming and are the result of festering relationships between people. People hate one another instead of having love for one another. This leads to hostilities and death as two mutually antagonistic entities engage in battle. When groups of people do not turn the other cheek, walk the extra mile, and turn over their tunic as well as there cloak, the result is war.

War can snowball into more than tragic events when peoples seek to retaliate and avenge themselves on their enemies. Vengeance and retaliation fuel the fires of war until only one side is left or the other side is completely exhausted and sues for peace. Perhaps there is hope that one side will be flexible and accept the jibes and taunts of the enemy and avert war. The problem is that if one side does not prepare for war then the other side will simply invade and take over. Perhaps being occupied is better than the death and destructions of war and there is always the possibility that the enemy will tire of occupation and return to their own country. It is certain that people will lose much if they engage in war. Without an attempt at peace people and property will be destroyed. If groups of people would only forgive their enemies without responding to perceived and real slights we might find a better world.

WARS

" Where do the wars and where do the conflicts among you come from? Is it not from your passions that make war within your members? You covet but you do not possess. You kill and envy but you cannot obtain; you fight and wage war. You do not possess because you do not ask. You ask but you do not receive, because you ask wrongly, to spend it on your passions."

James 4:1-3

JUST WARS

The word war is derived from the Teutonic werra which means confusion strife, and the German wirra which means confusion, disorder, and disturbance. It is a conflict carried out by force of arms as between nations or states or between parties within a state. It is a conflict carried on by force of arms or a series of battles or campaigns.

With war comes death and destruction. Men kill each other in contradiction to the commandment Thou shall not kill. When is war justified then? Is there ever a just war?

While war is rarely justified, it sometimes is. Just wars include war against people that promote genocide of another group of people or country. (Genocide that is not within God's will; there may be groups of people that are so evil so as to deserve genocide to include cultures that promote infanticide). If the party to be warred against is guilty of human oppression of a serious nature, is guilty of serious civil or human rights violations, then war is justified. War may be justified if one country or people denies another people access to food, clothing, water, or other basic elements necessary to live. However the war is justified only if the chances are good that the war can relieve the human suffering and human rights violations involved ie. that the human suffering caused by the war does not surpass that human suffering that already existed. Wars to protect liberty and freedom are always justified. Wars to protect innocents or prevent mass abortion is sometimes necessary.

There are circumstances when war is never justified. It is not just to war to steal natural resources from another people or country. War based on differences of race or supposed racial superiority are never justified. Again war based on differences in economic policies such as communism versus capitalism is never justified. Religious wars between churches are also unjustified as are wars between various religions that can live in peaceful coexistence.

Another aspect to the concept of just war is the participation of the individual soldier in a war. If the state or country declares another state or country an enemy and an individual soldier believes the war to be unjust, what is the responsibility of the individual soldier when called upon to kill an enemy combatant when his own life is a risk if he does not kill? The concepts here involve to right to self protection versus the commandant from God thou shall not kill. What is more important to protect your own life and in doing so kill another human being, or let yourself die and keep the commandment. The expression better a martyr that a murderer applies here.

Wars often cause so much economically and place such a toll on nations, cause so much death and destruction, and cause outrageous human suffering that it is possible to believe any war unjustified. In a nuclear age when the existence of the whole world is at stake the risks of war and potential benefits must be carefully weighed. Preemptive arms buildups to maintain the peace can be especially costly and divert human resources from other critical areas of human need and survival. So many times wars have been based not on moral grounds but on poor leadership or poor decisions made by masses of people.

" There is an appointed time for everything, and a time for every affair under the heavens.- A time to love and a time to hate; a time of war, and a time of peace"

Ecclesiastes 3:1, 8

WARS

There are a variety of reasons wars occur. Wars occur because of economic factors. When one country owes another country money and does not repay it, this is a factor to start a war. Or if there are excessive demands that reparations be paid. Or if one country blocks the trade of another country to block the importation or exportation of goods. Piracy may be included in this. External manipulation of a countries economy or money supply is also a cause of war

Another factor is religious difference or racial difference that leads to conflict. Simple hatred of another racial or religious group can and has led to war.

Thoughts of racial superiority or religious fanaticism often fan the flames of war.

Governments that oppress politically or economically have led to civil war. And denial of civil or human rights have led to war in the past. Tyranny by kings or theocracies has led to internal and external conflict.

Some peoples fight wars for status, the victor gains status in the world community and the defeated lose status. To gain possession of certain property has led to war. Examples here include the crusades to gain the Holy Land, or the Battle of Indians or Mexicans with the people of the United States to gain property for their country.

Some wars are familial in nature or when the countries leaders are related by blood and family arguments start. Woman are rarely a cause of war. When the leader of one country seeks a female of another ruler or a woman of another country who refuses to marry.

Wars are caused by differences of social and economic philosophies such as capitalism versus communism.

" There was a judge in a certain town who neither feared God nor respected any human being. And a widow in that town used to come to him and say, 'Render a just decision for me against my adversary.' For a long time the judge was unwilling, but eventually he thought, ' While it is true that I neither fear God nor respect and human being, because this widow keeps bothering me I shall deliver a just decision for her lest she finally come and strike me.'" The Lord said,"Pay attention to what the dishonest judge says. Will not God then secure the rights of his chosen ones who call out to him day and night? Will he be slow to answer them? I tell you, he will see to it that justice is done to them speedily."

Luke 18:2-8